MR. SKINNY

by Roger Hargreaves

Mr Skinny was extraordinarily thin.

Painfully thin.

If he turned sideways, you could hardly see him at all.

And, what made it even worse, was that he lived in a place called Fatland.

Yes, Fatland!

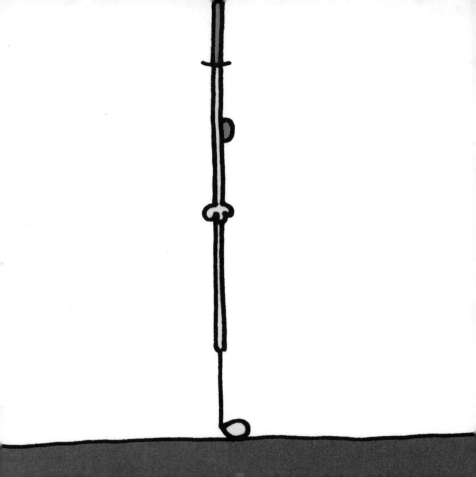

As you can very well imagine, everything and everybody in Fatland was as fat as could be.

Not stout.

Fat!

Fatland dogs were extremely fat!

Fatland worms were extraordinarily fat!

Fatland birds were exceedingly fat!

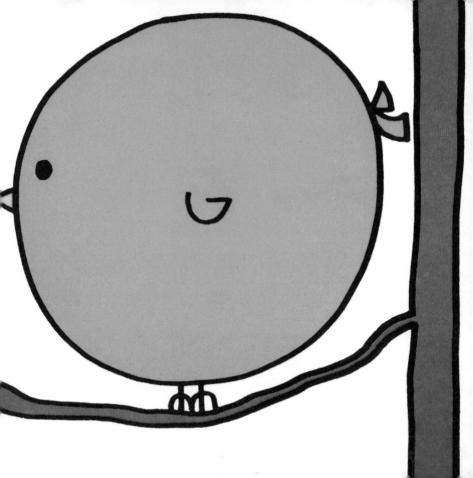

And you should see a Fatland elephant.

Phew!

And there, in the middle of all this fatness, lived Mr Skinny.

In the thinnest house you've ever seen.

Poor Mr Skinny, he didn't like being so different from everything and everybody.

But, there wasn't very much he could do about it.

You see, he had hardly any appetite at all.

A Mr Skinny meal was a very meagre affair.

Do you know what he had for breakfast?

One cornflake!

And for lunch?

One baked bean!

And for tea?

Nothing!

And for supper?

The world's smallest sausage!

And after that, he felt so full he went straight to bed.

In his long thin bed in his long thin bedroom in his long thin house, in Fatland.

"Oh, I do so wish I could do something about my appetite," he sighed to himself just before he went to sleep.

"I think," he thought, "that I had better go and see the doctor about it."

And he went to sleep.

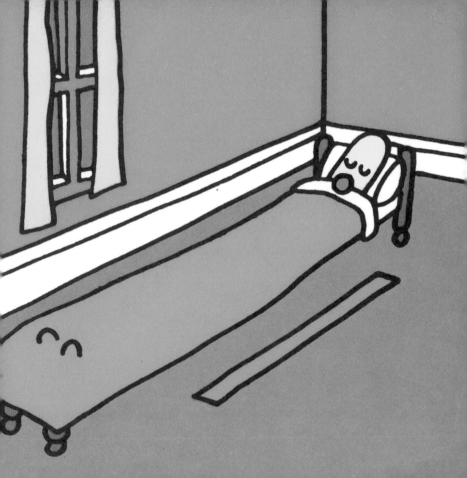

The following morning was lovely.

A large fat sun shone down on the fat green trees and the fat yellow flowers, and through them walked Mr Skinny on his way to see the doctor.

Doctor Plump!

"Come in, come in," he wheezed as Mr Skinny knocked at his door.

"Sit down, sit down," he wheezed as Mr Skinny entered.

"And what," he wheezed, putting his plump fingers together, "seems to be the trouble?"

"It's my appetite," explained Mr Skinny. "I'd like to be able to eat more so that I could put on a little weight."

"Yes, you are rather (how shall I put it) thin," wheezed the doctor, looking at him over his glasses.

"I know," he continued, "let's start the treatment right now!"

He licked his lips.

"This very moment," he added.

And he opened a drawer in his desk and took out an enormous cream cake.

He put it on the desk in front of him.

And opened another drawer and took out half a dozen doughnuts.

And put them on the desk in front of him.

And opened another drawer and took out a dozen currant buns.

And put them on the desk in front of him.

"Elevenses," he explained.

"But it's only 10 o'clock," said Mr Skinny.

"Who's counting?" wheezed Doctor Plump.

And without further ado, he and Mr Skinny ate the lot.

Mr Skinny ate a dab of cream, a doughnut crumb and one currant.

Doctor Plump ate the rest!

"Mmm," wheezed Doctor Plump, popping the last currant bun into his mouth, and looking at Mr Skinny.

"I see," he said, "what you mean about your appetite."

He thought for a moment.

"Only one thing for it," he wheezed. "This calls for drastic measures." And he picked up his telephone in his podgy fingers and dialled a number.

One hundred miles away, the telephone rang.

PRRR PRRR! PRRR PRRR!

"Hello," said a voice.

Do you know whose voice it was?

"Mr Greedy speaking," said the voice.

Mr Greedy listened to what Doctor Plump had to say.

"You'd like a Mr Skinny to come to stay?" he said.

"To build up his appetite?" he added.

"Delighted," he agreed.

And so, Mr Skinny went to stay with Mr Greedy.

He stayed for a month.

And, during that time, Mr Greedy did manage to increase Mr Skinny's appetite.

And so, at the end of the month, Mr Skinny returned home.

Happy!

With a tummy!

A tummy was something Mr Skinny had always wanted.

"I never knew I had it in me," he chuckled to himself.

He was feeling so proud of his tummy, he decided to call in and see Doctor Plump on his way home.

"I say," wheezed Doctor Plump, looking him up and down.

"Congratulations!"

"Tell you what," he went on. "This calls for a celebration!"

And he opened his desk drawer.

3 Great Offers for MR. MEN Fans!

MR. MEN TOKEN

1 New Mr. Men or Little Miss Library Bus Presentation Cases

A brand new stronger, roomier school bus library box, with sturdy carrying handle and stay-closed fasteners.
The full colour, wipe-clean boxes make a great home for your full collection.
They're just £5.99 inc P&P and free bookmark!

☐ MR. MEN ☐ LITTLE MISS (please tick and order overleaf)

2 Door Hangers and Posters

PLEASE STICK YOUR 50P COIN HERE

In every Mr. Men and Little Miss book like this one, you will find a special token. Collect 6 tokens and we will send you a brilliant Mr. Men or Little Miss poster and a Mr. Men or Little Miss double sided full colour bedroom door hanger of your choice. Simply tick your choice in the list and tape a 50p coin for your two items to this page.

Door Hangers (please tick)
☐ Mr. Nosey & Mr. Muddle
☐ Mr. Slow & Mr. Busy
☐ Mr. Messy & Mr. Quiet
☐ Mr. Perfect & Mr. Forgetful
☐ Little Miss Fun & Little Miss Late
☐ Little Miss Helpful & Little Miss Tidy
☐ Little Miss Busy & Little Miss Brainy
☐ Little Miss Star & Little Miss Fun

Posters (please tick)
☐ MR. MEN
☐ LITTLE MISS

3 Sixteen Beautiful Fridge Magnets – any 2 for £2.00!

inc.P&P

They're very special collector's items!
Simply tick your first and second* choices from the list below
of any 2 characters!

1st Choice

- ☐ Mr. Happy
- ☐ Mr. Lazy
- ☐ Mr. Topsy-Turvy
- ☐ Mr. Bounce
- ☐ Mr. Bump
- ☐ Mr. Small
- ☐ Mr. Snow
- ☐ Mr. Wrong

- ☐ Mr. Daydream
- ☐ Mr. Tickle
- ☐ Mr. Greedy
- ☐ Mr. Funny
- ☐ Little Miss Giggles
- ☐ Little Miss Splendid
- ☐ Little Miss Naughty
- ☐ Little Miss Sunshine

2nd Choice

- ☐ Mr. Happy
- ☐ Mr. Lazy
- ☐ Mr. Topsy-Turvy
- ☐ Mr. Bounce
- ☐ Mr. Bump
- ☐ Mr. Small
- ☐ Mr. Snow
- ☐ Mr. Wrong

- ☐ Mr. Daydream
- ☐ Mr. Tickle
- ☐ Mr. Greedy
- ☐ Mr. Funny
- ☐ Little Miss Giggles
- ☐ Little Miss Splendid
- ☐ Little Miss Naughty
- ☐ Little Miss Sunshine

*Only in case your first choice is out of stock.

TO BE COMPLETED BY AN ADULT

To apply for any of these great offers, ask an adult to complete the coupon below and send it with
the appropriate payment and tokens, if needed, to MR. MEN CLASSIC OFFER, PO BOX 715, HORSHAM RH12 5WG

☐ Please send ____ Mr. Men Library case(s) and/or ____ Little Miss Library case(s) at £5.99 each inc P&P

☐ Please send a poster and door hanger as selected overleaf. I enclose six tokens plus a 50p coin for P&P

☐ Please send me ____ pair(s) of Mr. Men/Little Miss fridge magnets, as selected above at £2.00 inc P&P

Fan's Name _____

Address _____

_____ **Postcode** _____

Date of Birth _____

Name of Parent/Guardian _____

Total amount enclosed £ _____

☐ **I enclose a cheque/postal order payable to Egmont Books Limited**

☐ **Please charge my MasterCard/Visa/Amex/Switch or Delta account** (delete as appropriate)

Card Number

Expiry date ___/___ **Signature** _____

MR.MEN   **LITTLE MISS**
Mr. Men and Little Miss™ & ©Mrs. Roger Hargreaves